S0-EAV-715

WITHDRAWN

LJHS IMC
1355 N 22
LARAMIE, WY 82070

RAOUL WALLENBERG: MISSING DIPLOMAT

by

Anita Larsen

Illustrated by
James Watling

CRESTWOOD HOUSE
NEW YORK

Maxwell Macmillan Canada
Toronto

Maxwell Macmillan International
New York Oxford Singapore Sydney

Library of Congress Cataloging-in-Publication Data
Larsen, Anita.

Raoul Wallenberg: missing diplomat / by Anita Larsen. — 1st ed.
p. cm. — (History's mysteries)
Includes bibliographical references and index.
Summary: A biography of the Swedish diplomat who helped save thousands of Hungarian Jews from the Nazis before mysteriously disappearing when the Russians occupied Budapest.
ISBN 0-89686-616-5
1. Wallenberg, Raoul—Juvenile literature. 2. World War, 1939-1945—Civilian relief—Hungary—Juvenile literature. 3. Holocaust, Jewish (1939-1945)—Hungary—Juvenile literature. 4. Jews—Hungary—History—20th century—Juvenile literature. 5. Diplomats—Sweden—Biography—Juvenile literature. 6. Righteous Gentiles in Holocaust—Biography—Juvenile literature. [1. Wallenberg, Raoul. 2. Diplomats. 3. World War, 1939-1945—Jews—Rescue. 4. Holocaust, Jewish (1939-1945)—Hungary.] I. Title. II. Series.
D809.S8W3252 1992
940.54'77943912'092—dc20
[B]

91-19937
CIP
AC

Crestwood House
Macmillan Publishing Company
866 Third Avenue
New York, NY 10022

Maxwell Macmillan Canada, Inc.
1200 Eglinton Avenue East
Suite 200
Don Mills, Ontario M3C 3N1

Macmillan Publishing Company is part of the Maxwell Communication Group of Companies.

First edition

Printed in the United States of America

10 9 8 7 6 5 4 3 2 1

CONTENTS

THE CASE OPENS

It is January 6, 1945. For the past weeks the Soviet army has laid siege to Budapest, the capital of Hungary. The city will soon fall.

Raoul Wallenberg, a 32-year-old Swedish junior diplomat, stands on Castle Hill, the highest point in Budapest. He has been driven there, past the bloated, rotting bodies of enemy soldiers and their Jewish forced laborers.

The lethal thunder of Russian bombs shakes the city. Russia fights for the Allied forces, which include the United States. Will the Soviets free Budapest or occupy it, Wallenberg wonders. But even Soviet occupation "is better than this," he tells his companion, referring to the carnage around them. It is the result of 12 weeks of Nazi terror in the streets.

Because Hungary is under German control, the

country fights for the Axis powers, which include Germany, Italy and Japan. When Budapest falls, the Nazi SS troops, Germany's elite security force, and their Hungarian counterparts, the Arrow Cross, will be defeated. The terror they have caused will end.

The horror has gone on for months. Hitler's plan to build a "master race" means that anyone who doesn't fit his ideal—Jews, gypsies, Poles, homosexuals and blacks—must be exterminated. Wallenberg has worked feverishly to save Hungarian Jews.

Since the middle of 1944, thousands of Hungarian Jews have died daily. Some were picked off the streets, beaten and shot. Others were marched to the banks of the Danube, the river that divides the city into two parts, Buda and Pest. Often three were tied together there and one was shot, dragging the other two into the water to drown. The Axis saved bullets this way.

On December 8, 1944, Wallenberg wrote to his mother, "I had thought to be home certainly for Christmas." But he was incapable of walking away from the desperate situation in Budapest.

In fact, no one from the Swedish legation returned home for Christmas in 1944. On Christmas Day, the neutral Swedish legation was attacked by the Hungarian Arrow Cross. Wallenberg escaped because he had already moved to a special "safe" building in the Jewish section, in Pest. His diplomatic papers were false anyway. He was really on assignment for the American War Refugee Board.

Working 20 hours a day, Wallenberg organized a staff of 350 workers and 40 doctors. He found and bribed informants. He rolled up in his big, black Studebaker to pluck Jews from death, giving them "Swedish passports" so they could escape. He set up safe houses.

The Jews called him Messiah and Angel of Rescue. The spiritual names fit him. Wallenberg's two-month assignment lasted nearly six months and grew into a zealous mission. That dedication is what made him great. It also destroyed him.

Wallenberg's success outraged the Arrow Cross. They were determined to kill him. Wallenberg recognized the danger but continued to operate in the deadly arena with wit and style. With the end of his rescue work in sight, he still looked ahead. The Angel of Rescue had dreams of becoming the master rebuilder of Hungary, according to Harvey Rosenfeld, author of *Wallenberg: Angel of Rescue.* Wallenberg told a co-worker, "It is true that the

Jews need my help now and will continue to do so after the war. But it is also true that the entire Hungarian nation will desperately need my assistance when peace comes." The Russians would—*must*—help.

When the Russians took control of Budapest, Wallenberg finished the final rescue details under their guard. He packed for a trip to Debrecen, a city in the northeast, to meet with high Russian officials. But his request for the meeting had confused the Soviets. They became suspicious of his motives.

Wallenberg said good-bye to his assistants on January 17, 1945. "I don't know whether I'm going as a prisoner or as a guest," Wallenberg said. He promised to return in a week.

But Raoul Wallenberg never returned from Debrecen. What happened to him?

THE CASE FILE

CITIZEN OF THE WORLD

Raoul Wallenberg was born on August 4, 1912, in Sweden. His mother, Maj, had been widowed three months before. She doted on her son but didn't coddle him. Convinced he was special, Maj encouraged Raoul's inquisitive spirit.

Today in Sweden, the Wallenbergs are still a part of the capitalist establishment. The family had become wealthy from its business and banking enterprises. It had gained power through foreign service and its work for the church and in politics.

At eight, Raoul had memorized great portions of the *Nordic Encyclopedia.* He also had memorized the annual reports of major Swedish companies. Most of them were part of the Wallenberg empire, so it was just another way to learn about his family.

When Raoul was 11 his grandfather was appointed ambassador to Turkey. He sent for the boy to visit him there. It was Raoul's first major trip alone.

By now, Maj had married Fredrick von Dardel, who treated Raoul like a son even after his own children, Guy and Nina, were born. It was Raoul's half brother, Guy, who discovered one day while coloring that Raoul was color-blind. People who were color-blind couldn't serve in the navy. Raoul Wallenberg would have to find another way to serve his country as Wallenbergs were expected to do.

Raoul had a remarkable skill for learning languages. As a teen, he spoke English, French and German fluently. This was part of Grandfather Gustav's educational scheme for Raoul.

Another part of that scheme was the "American experience." Gustav wanted Raoul to have the benefits of an American education. But he thought schools on the East Coast of the United States were elitist. He wanted Raoul to meet a broad range of people. So at 19 Raoul began work on an undergraduate degree in architecture at the University of Michigan in Ann Arbor.

Ann Arbor was too small a town for Raoul. He hitchhiked to the West Coast and to Mexico, reporting his trips to his grandfather. "I went 300 miles on 50 cents," he wrote. But the real value of hitchhiking was the "great practice it offers one in the art of diplomacy and negotiating. You have to be on your guard."

Raoul graduated from Ann Arbor with honors.

He made friends easily and quickly, but he had no special friend. He was a loner.

In 1936 Raoul was sent to Haifa, Palestine, for financial training. Something other than finances touched him there—the stories he heard from Jewish beggars who had once been prosperous Germans. In Germany Jews had been stripped of all their rights. Their possessions had been taken from them, and they'd been expelled from their homeland.

In the spring of 1937 Raoul's grandfather suddenly died. Raoul, groomed for success, also needed a sponsor in his social class in Sweden. He no longer had one. His godfather, Jacob, and Uncle Marcus had their own grandchildren.

Jacob gave Raoul a series of temporary assignments at his bank. None of them led to anything. Finally a friend of Jacob's put Raoul in touch with a Hungarian businessman named Kalman Lauer. Lauer was a Jew. It was dangerous for Jews to travel. Lauer needed someone who could operate freely to help him. He needed a troubleshooter to take his place. Wallenberg took the job—traveling, negotiating and studying the psychology of different peoples. He became more of a citizen of the world then before. The job was good training for the important work that was to come.

THE MISSION

In early 1942 the Nazis were increasing the systematic murder of Jews. Special Nazi SS units were organized to round up Jews and "resettle" them in death camps. By 1943 Auschwitz had been set up as an extermination camp. Located in Poland, it was too far from the Allied forces' bombing runs to destroy, according to Allied military commanders. This allowed the Nazis freedom to kill the imprisoned Jews.

The enormity of the slaughter was staggering. A telegram of October 18, 1944, sent to Berlin from Hitler's ambassador to Budapest, describes the efficiency of the Nazi plan to exterminate the Jews: "Total number of Jews in Hungary on March 19 of this year, about 800,000. Already transported into the territory of the Reich, about 430,000. Jewish work force of the Hungarian Army, about 150,000. In the region of Budapest, about 200,000." Most of these people would die. By 1944 the only surviving Jewish community was in Hungary. Before the war, it had been the third largest in Europe.

In 1944, nearly the end of the war, President Franklin D. Roosevelt had organized a War Refugee Board and had empowered it to work. The board sent a man to Sweden to hire someone to initiate a

Hungarian rescue effort. The man had no luck until he ran into Kalman Lauer in an elevator.

"I know the man for the job," Lauer said. "His name is Wallenberg."

Wallenberg got a call from the refugee board to be interviewed for the job. It was a warm summer day, and he was leading war maneuvers. Although Sweden was neutral, Wallenberg did not think this meant blanket protection from the German threat. As a result, he had volunteered to be an instructor in the Swedish National Guard. During this time he had honed his shooting skills and built up stamina and strength.

Wallenberg was so eager for the job no one else wanted that he told the refugee board interviewer he was half Jewish. He wasn't. But this mission was worthy of one of the Wallenberg Big Men.

Raoul made demands, though. He wanted a diplomatic passport and money for bribes and expenses. Those demands were met. He spent his last two days in Stockholm reading secret reports and creating a communications code. He knew the Germans had already cracked Swedish diplomatic codes.

Then Wallenberg bought a secondhand revolver and stuffed two knapsacks with reports and names of contacts in Budapest.

Wallenberg arrived in Budapest on July 9, 1944. He sent his first report only days later, on July 17. His report included the following facts: Sealed boxcars carried 75 to 80 persons, along with some bread, a pail of water and a pail for sanitation. In the Nazi gas chambers 6,000 people were exterminated daily. Only 200,000 Jews were still alive in Budapest. Hungarian leaders wanted to stop the deportations. They were hampered by German control and their own political squabbles.

Wallenberg sent his second report the next day, July 18. He had discovered an informant, who had escaped from Auschwitz to tell of torturous medical experiments performed on prisoners. Christians were hiding 20,000 to 50,000 Jews in Budapest. In the first week of July, many Jews had been baptized as Christians for their own protection. Many Hungarians blamed the Germans for the savagery against the Jews, but were themselves prejudiced toward them. They thought the Jews were the reason no nation had helped Hungary when the country was taken over by German sympathizers.

On July 19, Wallenberg sent a letter outlining his rescue plans. Some of these plans broke laws, but he wasn't bothered by that.

What did bother Wallenberg was the defeated attitude of the Jews themselves.

Wallenberg found himself with two missions: One was to rescue Jews. The other was to revitalize the Jews' will to survive.

"ANGEL OF RESCUE"

Not all Jews, however, accepted a fate at the hands of the Nazis. From those who could still fight, Wallenberg recruited his assistants. He formed a special Section C within the Swedish diplomatic legation to help him organize relief efforts and administer rescues. He expected long hours and complete dedication from his recruits. In return he negotiated with the Hungarians so that his co-workers did not have to wear yellow stars or live in marked houses.

What Wallenberg expected of others, he expected of himself. He hunted for shoes for an old people's home. He planned menus for his soup kitchen. He loaded supply trucks. And he set his rescue plan in motion. His plan was clever and dramatic.

First, Wallenberg issued protective passports. He had to convince Hungarian officials to approve the passports. For a Jew to qualify, all that was needed was any kind of link with a Swedish citizen. A passport entitled its bearer to a trip to Sweden, which none of the holders ever intended to make. Soon the Swiss legation picked up the idea and began issuing their own passports, which they called "Palestine passes."

But the Swedish passports were more effective because they looked official. They had a stamped signature of the Swedish minister and a photograph of the bearer. These passports were easily forged. To make a false passport, it was necessary only to change the photograph and duplicate the passport itself. There was a lively black market in these fabricated passports. Some people paid as much as $5,000 for one.

Wallenberg's next step was to find separate housing for the "international" Jews, as those carrying the passes Wallenberg had given them were called. Wallenberg also bought and rented houses in the former Jewish quarter. Immediately the blue-and-yellow Swedish flag was hung there, showing that the houses were diplomatic property. This meant they couldn't be invaded or plundered. This idea also spread to diplomats from other neutral countries. Soon there was a protected international ghetto in Budapest—a city within a city.

Wallenberg also called on the regent of Hungary. The regent was the head of state; Wallenberg was merely a first secretary from a neutral country. But by the time the meeting ended, Wallenberg had convinced the regent that he should ease up on the Jews in Budapest.

By mid-September Jews began removing their yellow stars. No one stopped them. Jewish confidence was growing. But so was German uneasiness. To complicate matters, the Russian army was advancing and the Hungarian regent was becoming independent of German authority. He had even agreed to a peace with the Russians!

On October 15, 1944, the Germans kidnapped the regent's son. They told the regent to call off the Russian armistice if he wanted to see his son again. The regent agreed. But a radio announcement of the armistice was so far along that it couldn't be stopped. All of Budapest heard it, and the city exploded with joy.

The Nazis swiftly moved in. By the time the crowds now celebrating in the streets heard the armistice announcement the second time, German tanks were in place. The regent was exiled to Germany and replaced by the Hungarian Arrow Cross forces. Nazi gestapo moved in to support

them. Adolf Eichmann, Hitler's trusted killer, returned to the city.

The Hungarian Arrow Cross began a blood bath the day after the regent left. One of their "games" of torture was to pull a Jew from a work gang or deportation line, search him for money, strip him, put him in a barrel and then fill the barrel with water. Because it was winter the person and the water quickly froze into a block of ice. Then the barrel was passed around so other Jews could see the horror.

These terrors spurred Wallenberg to renew his efforts. His staff worked around the clock. Wallenberg himself began negotiations, using all the skills he'd amassed. He was able to see what an official wanted. Then he traded that protection for the people he was trying to rescue.

EICHMANN'S PROBLEM

Efficient human slaughter on a massive scale proved to be a problem for Eichmann to organize effectively. Vehicles used to transport Jews were needed to repel the Russians. So in early November 1944, Eichmann decided the Jews could walk the 125 miles from Budapest to Auschwitz. These became death marches.

At the gateway to Auschwitz, Eichmann waited with an assistant for the Jews to arrive. When the exhausted prisoners had straggled in, the Nazis counted heads.

Wallenberg's response to the death marches was to initiate what the Jews called "flying squadron" rescues.

At the end of one of the first marches, Wallenberg showed up, shouting, "I demand those with Swedish passports to raise them high!" Eichmann and his head counter were caught off guard. But so were the marchers. "You there!" Wallenberg shouted, pointing to one surprised Jew. "Get in that line!" That line led to International Red Cross trucks that would take the Jews back to Budapest. "And you!" Wallenberg pointed to another astonished Jew. "Get behind him. I know I issued you a passport."

And so it went, until several hundred Jews had been transferred to Wallenberg's convoy. Wallenberg's bluff worked because Eichmann hated public confrontations.

Wallenberg took to the road too. He and a group of aides drove along the route of the march, then stopped and snatched people from the line. Wallenberg would flash Swedish protective papers—or even a blank book—and scream like an enraged German authority: "These are my own initials! This is a Swede!" The Germans responded to authority. They believed Wallenberg simply because he seemed convincing.

Eichmann still struggled to solve his overwhelming problem of liquidating the Jews. Time was running short, and the "Jew-dog," as he called Wallenberg, was causing trouble. So Eichmann drew up plans for a walled central ghetto to hold all surviving Jews. It was to follow the model of the Warsaw ghetto in Poland. All the Christians in one section were moved out. Then the Jews were herded in and kept there.

The Russians began their siege of Budapest on December 8, 1944. On December 23 Eichmann fled. Arrow Cross leadership had left even earlier. But between December 8 and 23, 60,000 Jews had been placed in the central ghetto.

There were still 30,000 Jews living in the protected international ghetto. The Arrow Cross, now leaderless, raided any house they wished. Wallenberg couldn't stop them.

THE RUSSIANS ARE COMING!

By the first week of January 1945, the Russians

had surrounded Budapest. But the transfer of Jews to the central ghetto continued. Varying reports indicate that from 12,000 to 15,000 Christians who previously lived there were replaced by 63,000 to 90,000 Jews.

Whatever the number, the threat of imminent starvation inside the ghetto was a great concern. Arrow Cross authorities told Wallenberg not to worry. The ghetto inhabitants would "be exterminated with machine guns in due time," one said. Now Wallenberg worked even more feverishly.

But Wallenberg was also being hunted. An Arrow Cross official had defected and come to work with Wallenberg. He informed Wallenberg of death plots against him. Wallenberg said, "I'm not going to take any more care of my person than I do of my signatures." He was now signing passports for anyone who asked for them.

He returned to the negotiating table and managed to stop further transfers of Jews. He gained other concessions as well.

His bargaining chip was food. There was almost no food in Budapest now.

Another bargaining chip was the power Raoul Wallenberg's actions had gained for his name. The Wallenberg name had come to stand for something far greater than the family wealth.

But nothing could stop the growing number of death threats on Wallenberg's life. He went into hiding. Then, almost magically, he would appear whenever he was needed. Wallenberg ended up at the headquarters of the Red Cross, where he would be one of the first to take part in the liberation of Budapest. For three days he slept and began laying the groundwork for a plan to rebuild Hungary.

THE RUSSIANS ARE HERE!

Meanwhile, the first wave of Russians invaded the janitors' ground-floor apartments throughout Budapest. They called the janitors "bourgeois," meaning that they were capitalists. In these first days of Joseph Stalin's Communist regime, the Russians hated capitalists.

The Hungarians were liberated from German occupation only to be devastated by Russian savagery. Since the Hungarians had been Germany's last ally, the Russians saw them as enemies. Civilians became prisoners of war and were marched off to Russian work camps. A new, provisional government under Russian control was quickly set up in Debrecen.

The Russians scoured the city. They crawled

through the air-raid shelters that connected through the cellars of buildings. They reached the international ghetto on January 16 and the central ghetto on January 17. Remaining Arrow Cross soldiers and Nazis tried to shoot their way out of the central ghetto, using living Jews as shields. Three thousand Jews died in this way. Another 250 rotting bodies were found in the central ghetto. But 100,000 Jews survived!

These survivors knocked down the walls of their prison. Outside, the beautiful city they remembered was a smoking heap of rubble and ashes.

On the morning of January 13, 1945, a Russian street patrol found Wallenberg in the cellar of one of his mission centers. Wallenberg had already begun studying Russian.

The Russians asked what he was doing in Budapest and why he was not with the other Swedish diplomats. Wallenberg answered their questions and then insisted on speaking to the highest Soviet authority. Confused, the Russians agreed to take him and his driver, Vilmos Langfelder, to their headquarters in Budapest.

The next day, Wallenberg and Langfelder returned to the mission center to pick up their belongings. A Russian officer was with them.

Wallenberg left instructions to keep the rescue operation going. He said he would return in a week. Then he and Langfelder drove off for Debrecen. They were escorted by Soviet motorcycles with sidecars. Neither man ever returned.

WALLENBERG: DEAD OR ALIVE?

The liberation Hungary hoped for had been denied them months before the Russians came. On October 15, 1944, Winston Churchill had negotiated the country away to the Soviets. As a result, members of the Swedish legation in Budapest were processed through Soviet internment camps. They arrived home in Stockholm by ship from Leningrad on April 18, 1945.

After their experiences, the returning diplomats did not share the fear of Russia other Swedes felt at the time. Naughty Swedish children were often told, "Careful, or the Russians will get you!"

Sweden wanted neutrality based on its prewar relations with Russia. When a Russian radio broadcast from Budapest announced that Wallenberg was "most probably assassinated by agents of the Gestapo," Swedish diplomats sighed with relief. They wouldn't have to argue with the Russians for Wallenberg's return.

Swedish diplomats had been worried about such an argument since January 16, 1945. That's the date of a Soviet deputy foreign minister's official note to the Swedish envoy in Moscow: "First Secretary Raoul Wallenberg of the Swedish legation in Budapest has gone over to the Russian side. Wallenberg and his belongings have been taken under Soviet protective custody."

But what Sweden didn't know was that Russia had changed under Stalin's rule. Anyone suspected of being a threat to the Russian state was put into prison by the NKVD, the Soviet secret police. The NKVD was like a state within a state. It made its own laws.

Inmates were thrown into windowless cells in the NKVD's vast prison system. The prisoners were dehumanized and put in virtual storage until it suited the Soviet state to release them or charge and sentence them.

Occasionally prisoners were sent to punishing work camps in the gulags, a network of labor camps in the far north and Siberia. By 1946 there were 15 million prisoners in the gulags.

When Wallenberg and his driver left Budapest, they were under NKVD arrest. With the defeat of the Nazis, the cold war that pitted Soviet

Communists against the West had begun.

The Soviets did not want a "messiah" like Wallenberg in Hungary. And Wallenberg was hated for his capitalist family. On the other hand he was a good asset for trading if a Soviet spy should ever be arrested in Sweden.

The Soviets thought Wallenberg was probably a spy himself. That was even more reason to keep him. The Soviets were convinced that members of Jewish organizations who had provided support for Wallenberg's rescue mission were plotting to kill Stalin. Also, members of Wallenberg's family had had business ties with Germany. The Russians feared the Germans even more than the Swedes feared the Russians.

The upshot was this statement issued by the Soviet foreign minister in August 1947: "Raoul Wallenberg is not in the Soviet Union, and he is unknown to us."

But released prisoners reported that Wallenberg was, in fact, in various Soviet prisons. They had either seen him or had exchanged messages with him, tapped out in prison code. These reports have been collected in Sweden in a long series of records called the White Book. They show that Wallenberg and Langfelder were first sent to Lubyanka prison in Moscow. There they were separated.

Wallenberg's movements through the prison system indicates that the Russians truly didn't know what to do with him. He was moved constantly, always kept off balance, always treated as a special case. "They just want me to disappear. Simply vanish into the night. That would suit them best," Wallenberg reportedly tapped in prison code.

Until Stalin died in 1953, the Soviets denied holding Wallenberg. The new Soviet administration outlawed the NKVD. On February 6, 1957, the official Soviet position on Wallenberg did an about-face. A memo dated July 17, 1947, said that prisoner "Walenberg," misspelling his name, had suffered a fatal heart attack in his cell on July 16, 1947.

Wallenberg had "come to life" only to die!

But sightings of Wallenberg continued. In fact, former prisoners were arrested again after saying they'd seen Wallenberg after 1947. The Swede had become a legend, a myth, and now a different kind of problem for the Russians.

If Wallenberg were freed, the Soviets would lose what they had gained in Hungary. They didn't want that. Hungary was now a Russian province, and the Russians wanted no disruptions in governing it. The official Soviet position returned

to a previous one. Russia, officials said, knew nothing about Wallenberg. Wallenberg had been lost once again!

But reports of sightings continued to come. Some said that Wallenberg was in solitary confinement. One said he had been seen going to his weekly bath under armed guard.

The most convincing proof that Wallenberg was alive came from a Dr. Nanna Svartz in 1961. A prominent Swedish physician and researcher, Dr. Svartz had gone to Moscow to attend an international medical congress. A colleague told her Wallenberg was in a mental hospital, where the Soviets often place political prisoners.

Dr. Svartz rushed from the medical congress to make plans to take Wallenberg home. But the necessary officials were on vacation. When she returned to the meetings, she was told the matter had to be handled through diplomatic channels.

Neither Swedish nor Soviet diplomats seemed interested in opening those channels. In fact, the official Russian position returned to an earlier view, that Wallenberg had died of a heart attack in prison in 1947. The official Swedish position was neutral.

The next big break in the case came when famed Nazi-hunter Simon Wiesenthal got involved.

Wallenberg's mother, who had searched for years for her son, took heart.

But Wiesenthal's search also failed. Continuing reports of a frail "old Swede" were investigated, but they led only to dead ends. Separating reality from legend was growing harder as the years passed.

The cold war thawed over the years. By the 1980s, Soviet-American relations were surprisingly warm. The Wallenberg case was mentioned again. But no answers were offered then or in the early 1990s.

You have just read the known facts about one of HISTORY'S MYSTERIES. To date, there have been no more answers to the mysteries posed in the story. There are possibilities, though. Read on and see which answer seems the most believable to you. How would you solve the case?

SOLUTIONS

GESTAPO VICTIM

Raoul Wallenberg and his driver were killed on their way to Debrecen. Retreating Nazi SS and Arrow Cross soldiers finally made good on their death threats. Eyewitness reports of the last days of World War II clearly show the desperation of the Axis forces. As it became clear the Russians would take Budapest, gestapo assassination attempts grew more determined, racking up a growing number of near-misses on Wallenberg.

Swedish diplomats didn't press for Wallenberg's release because they thought he was dead. A Russian radio announcement from Budapest concerning his death had been confirmed through diplomatic channels.

The series of conflicting Soviet reports about Wallenberg was due to internal turmoil. The Soviets constantly adjusted their story to meet their own needs. The sightings of Wallenberg reported by released Soviet political prisoners cannot be trusted.

HEART-ATTACK VICTIM

There is no reason to disbelieve the 1947 memo reporting the death of prisoner "Walenberg." That prisoner was, in fact, Raoul Wallenberg.

He and Langfelder were under NKVD arrest even before they left Budapest for Debrecen. Wallenberg was color-blind and couldn't recognize the red badges on the NKVD uniforms. He was just as eager to get Russian help in rebuilding Hungary as he had been to rescue Jews. He wouldn't have resisted being taken to Moscow.

Wallenberg had been in good physical shape from his Swedish National Guard training, but his demanding schedule in Budapest had exhausted him.

He was processed into the dehumanizing Soviet prison system. Months dragged on. No help from Sweden came. The Russians laughed at his plan to rebuild Hungary. He was put in "storage," unable to do anything. Finally it got to him, and he suffered a heart attack.

Released prisoner reports of sightings refer to another Swede, not Wallenberg. The changes in the official Soviet position over the years were simply political maneuvers.

SOVIET PRISON VICTIM

There is every reason to believe the sightings of Raoul Wallenberg made by released Soviet prisoners. They have had nothing to gain by making up a story about a man whose own country couldn't—or wouldn't—help him.

The White Book, a series of reports on Wallenberg, shows that for many years Sweden was uncertain whether Wallenberg was alive or dead. It is the largest file on an individual in the Swedish foreign office. The record indicates Wallenberg's continued energy. He was an inveterate "tapper," sending messages to other prisoners in prison code.

We also have ample proof of the man's invincible spirit. His actions in his "flying squadron" rescues in Hungary show that he was confident and determined. He wanted to be a Big Man, one of the family achievers, which gave him a strong motivation to live.

Even so, by 1992 Wallenberg would have been a Russian prisoner for over 45 years. If alive now he would be in his eighties. Few Soviet prisoners last that long. Raoul Wallenberg probably died at a place and time the world will never learn.

CLOSING THE CASE FILE

Raoul Wallenberg's case is a story of squalid political intrigue from every side. It is so complicated that every humanitarian impulse became entangled in deceit.

In 1948 citizens of Budapest sponsored the building of a huge monument of Saint George slaying the dragon as a memorial to Wallenberg. The Russians removed the monument the night before it was to be unveiled. The statue—minus the pedestal bearing the dedication and a relief of Wallenberg's face—was later erected outside a penicillin factory near Debrecen. The dedication and relief were never seen again. Raoul Wallenberg may not have made it to Debrecen, but his statue did.

Wallenberg was nominated in 1948 for a Nobel Peace Prize. He had become a very Big Man indeed.

CHRONOLOGY

1912	August 4, Raoul Wallenberg is born.
1936	Wallenberg, in Haifa, Palestine, hears stories from Jews of forced emigration.
1937	Wallenberg's grandfather dies.
1944	July 9, Swedish junior diplomat Wallenberg arrives in Budapest on American War Refugee Board assignment. July 19, Wallenberg outlines his rescue plan. early November Eichmann begins death marches. December 8, Soviet army begins siege of Budapest. December 23, Eichmann flees Budapest. December 24, Arrow Cross attacks Swedish legation.
1945	January 13, Russians reach Wallenberg. January 14, Wallenberg leaves for Debrecen. January 16, Russians reach international ghetto. January 17, Russians reach central ghetto. Soviet prisoners' claims to have seen Wallenberg begin.
1947	July 17, "Walenberg" heart-attack memo is made public.

RESOURCES

SOURCES

Lester, Elenore. *Wallenberg: The Man in the Iron Web.* Englewood Cliffs, N.J.: Prentice-Hall, 1982.
Marton, Kati. *Wallenberg.* New York: Random House, 1982.
Rosenfeld, Harvey. *Raoul Wallenberg: Angel of Rescue.* Buffalo, N. Y.: Prometheus Books, 1982.
Solzhenitsyn, Aleksandr. *The Gulag Archipelago.* New York: Harper & Row: Vol. 1, 1973; Vol. 2, 1975; Vol. 3, 1976.

FURTHER READING FOR YOUNG READERS

Friedman, Ina. *The Other Victims: First-Person Stories of Non-Jews Persecuted by the Nazis.* Boston: Houghton-Mifflin, 1990.
Meltzer, Milton. *Ain't Gonna Study War No More.* New York: Harper & Row, 1985.
Treseder, Terry Walton. *Hear, O Israel: A Story of the Warsaw Ghetto.* New York: Atheneum, 1990.

INDEX